MINDSET MATTERS

Thank you for always having a
GONNA-GET-IT-DONE mindset, Nancy Roberts. – Bryan

Written by
Bryan Smith

Illustrated by ## Lisa Griffin

BOYS TOWN
Press

Boys Town, Nebraska

Mindset Matters
Text and Illustrations Copyright © 2017 by Father Flanagan's Boys' Home
ISBN: 978-1-944882-12-9

Published by the Boys Town Press
14100 Crawford St.
Boys Town, NE 68010

For a Boys Town Press catalog, call **1-800-282-6657**
or visit our website: **BoysTownPress.org**

Publisher's Cataloging-in-Publication Data

Names: Smith, Bryan (Bryan Kyle), 1978- author. | Griffin, Lisa M. (Lisa Middleton), 1972- illustrator.

Title: Mindset matters / written by Bryan Smith ; illustrated by Lisa Griffin.

Description: Boys Town, NE : Boys Town Press, [2017] | Series: Without limits. | Audience: grades K-5. | Summary: At the first sign of trouble, Amelia frets she's a failure. But she soon learns that success has many definitions. "Mindset Matters" teaches children how to see problems and dilemmas as opportunities to learn and grow and reveals why failing doesn't make them failures.--Publisher.

Identifiers: ISBN: 978-1-944882-12-9

Subjects: LCSH: Failure (Psychology) in children--Juvenile fiction. | Fear of failure--Juvenile fiction. | Success in children--Juvenile fiction. | Problem solving in children--Juvenile fiction. | Self-reliance in children--Juvenile fiction. | Self-esteem in children--Juvenile fiction. | Emotions in children--Juvenile fiction. | Child psychology--Juvenile fiction. | Children--Life skills guides--Juvenile fiction. | CYAC: Failure (Psychology)--Fiction. | Success--Fiction. | Problem solving --Fiction. | Self-reliance--Fiction. | Self-esteem--Fiction. | Emotions--Fiction. | Conduct of life-- Fiction. | BISAC: JUVENILE FICTION / Social Themes / Emotions & Feelings. | JUVENILE FICTION / Social Themes / New Experience. | JUVENILE FICTION / Social Themes / Self- Esteem & Self-Reliance. | EDUCATION / Counseling / General.

Classification: LCC: PZ7.S643366 M56 2017 | DDC: [Fic]--dc23

Printed in the United States
10 9 8 7 6 5 4 3 2

Boys Town Press is the publishing division of Boys Town, a national organization serving children and families.

Hey everyone. My name's Amelia, and I'm in 2nd grade.

My parents always help my little brother, Kevin, but today was going to be my turn.

It all started with something that was supposed to be fun – putting up our new swing set. Just so you know, not an easy thing to do.

I was getting really frustrated so I threw my hammer down and shouted,

"I QUIT!"

Dad said, *"What's wrong?"*

I yelled, **"UGH! Building things is for boys, and I'll NEVER be any good at it!"**

4

Dad told me I needed to have a better mindset.

"Very funny Dad. It's called a swing set, not a mindset. There's nothing wrong with the swing set. **It's me.** I'm just **NOT GOOD** at building things."

"No honey, mindset has to do with what you believe you can achieve. Some people have negative mindsets and always come up with excuses. I call that a **DOWN-IN-THE-DUMPS** mindset.

Other people stay with difficult things and find a way to get them done. I call that a **GONNA-GET-IT-DONE** mindset."

6

DOWN IN THE DUMPS

Let's Go!

X *I'll never be good at that.*

X Negative attitude

X Excuses

GONNA GET IT DONE

✓ *I'm not good at that...***YET.**

✓ Positive attitude

✓ Determined

7

Dad continued, "The first time I tried to build something with your grandpa, I smacked myself on the thumb with a hammer while trying to hit a nail. After that, it took me years before I really felt confident in building things. Throughout that whole time, I kept a **GONNA-GET-IT-DONE** mindset."

OUCH! It hurts so bad!

"It wasn't **IF** I was ever going to be good but rather **WHEN** I was going to be good at building things," Dad said. "I know it can be frustrating, but there are some steps you can follow to try to improve your **GONNA-GET-IT-DONE** mindset."

Dad said, "To have a **GONNA-GET-IT-DONE** mindset you should:

GONNA GET IT DONE

1. Imagine yourself completing the task.

2. If it's difficult, remind yourself "I may not be good at that... YET. But hard work pays off!"

3. Keep a positive attitude.

4. Keep on working until YOU reach that goal!

Amelia, if you can follow these steps, you'll be on track every time you try something new!" Dad said.

"So, Amelia, think about this question before you answer it. Are you going to be able to build this swing set?"

I paused for a minute before answering, **"NES."**

"What in the world does 'NES' mean?"

"It means No and Yes. It basically means I have no clue."

"No, Amelia, you need to believe in yourself and have a **GONNA-GET-IT-DONE** mindset."

10

Dad smiled and said, "When I ask if you can build it, remember the steps we just went over. If you say yes, it doesn't mean it's going to be easy but, in the end, you'll stick with it and find a way to put it together."

11

"Let's try this question again. Amelia, can you build this swing set?"

"Absolutely!

This swing set doesn't know who it's messing with. Let's win this battle. Just give me one minute so I can go put on some of Mom's makeup."

"Amelia, you don't need to get dressed up for this job."

Dad had no clue what I was doing. After a while, I came out in the backyard with makeup that looked like war paint. It took us almost **six hours** to build the swing set, but we got the job done. I guess Dad was right about hard work paying off.

Maybe there's something to this **GONNA-GET-IT-DONE** mindset thing after all! Dad even suggested I take a quick brain break when I got frustrated. I wonder if all of this could help me with math? That's one thing, no matter what I do, I am always terrible at. *I guess it's worth a try!*

13

The next day at school, it didn't take long before I got to one of those impossible math problems again.

Ding Dong...
nobody's home.
My brain's on vacation.

My teacher, Mrs. Moody, could tell I was frustrated and came over to me. She asked if I had ever heard of a **GONNA-GET-IT-DONE** mindset. "Uh, yeah." Were she and my dad working as a team?

Mrs. Moody asked what I could do to help get the problem solved. "I could look on someone else's paper!"

"Nice try, but that's called cheating," she said. "Think of something else."

I wish I could have but of course my mind went blank again, so I just laid my head down on my desk.

15

Mrs. Moody talked to me more about having a **GONNA-GET-IT-DONE** mindset. She reminded me of the steps and helped me come up with some ways to help the situation.

GONNA GET IT DONE

1. Imagine yourself completing the task.

2. If it's difficult, remind yourself "I may not be good at that... YET. But hard work pays off!"

3. Keep a positive attitude.

4. Keep on working until **YOU** reach that goal!

I decided I wanted to work with Mrs. Moody. She showed me a few ways to solve the math problem and even drew a picture to show how to solve it.

The following day, another one of those impossible math problems showed up again but this time I had a different mindset. **"Boy do I feel sorry for this problem,"** I thought. **"It doesn't stand a chance against me!"** I solved it right away and even drew a picture to prove my answer. When it comes to math problems, **I'M GONNA GET THEM DONE!**

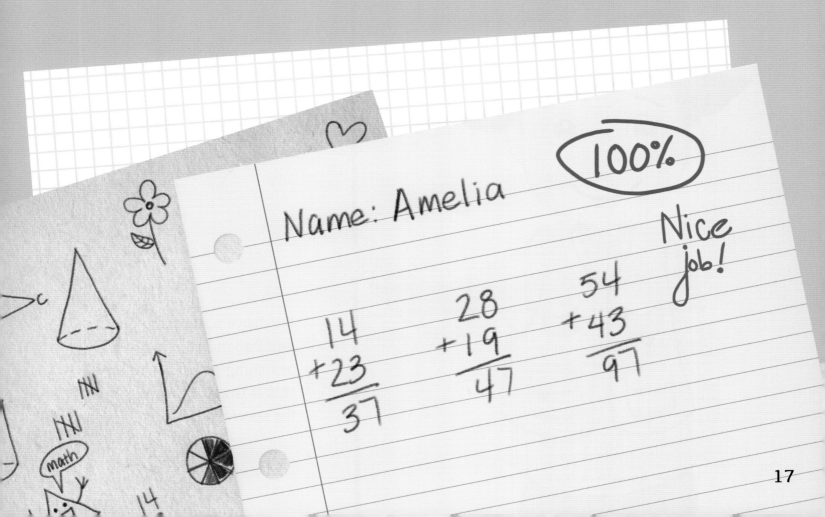

I guess my teacher told Dad what a great job I did because right when I walked in the door, Dad said, **"Hey guys, jump in the car. We're going to celebrate Amelia's great day at school."**

We drove up to some pond, and Dad pulled out a bunch of fishing poles. "Amelia, this is the place I take Kevin for special occasions."

I had never been fishing, but I sure wanted to try. It didn't seem too hard. Dad threw the line out, and I got to pull it in. **NOTHING!**

We did this 10 more times and the same thing happened every time...**NOTHING!** What was the point of this? Dad saw my frustration and said, "Just wait. All it takes is one catch and you'll be hooked."

That's when it happened.

As I was reeling in the line, I felt a huge tug. I fought and fought and fought. This fish was going to be

HUGE!

As I pulled it out of the water, Kevin yelled, "Hey, nice stick!" I couldn't believe I caught a stick instead of a fish. "I HATE fishing. I'm never going to catch a fish. I have no idea how to fish."

Once again, Dad talked to me about a **GONNA-GET-IT-DONE** mindset. "Amelia, you don't know how to catch a fish...YET. But if you stick with it, I think I can help." Dad told me I was pulling the line in too fast, and I needed to bait the hook without the tip showing. Soon after, I was posing for a photo with my first fish. This **GONNA-GET-IT-DONE** mindset worked again!

That weekend was my brother's birthday. He got this really cool skateboard as a gift. It wasn't long before I had to step in and explain the **GONNA-GET-IT-DONE** mindset.

Whoa!

I QUIT!

Nooooooo!

Kevin tried to ride the skateboard
three or four times but fell flat
on his face every time. "I hate
this skateboard," he screamed.

"I QUIT!"

23

I talked to Kevin about having a **GONNA-GET-IT-DONE** mindset.
He asked if I knew how to ride a skateboard.

Of course I fell several times, but
I was not going to give up. Each time,
I stayed on longer and went further.

25

It wasn't long before I rode down the whole street
without falling off. Right away, Kevin said,

"If you can do it, I can too."

"Now there's that **GONNA-GET-IT-DONE** mindset I knew you had,"
Dad said as he watched us.

Yii

By the end of the day, we could both ride as far as a football field. Dad was really proud of us. **"Dad, you should give it a try!"** I said. He jumped on the skateboard and immediately fell flat on his face. "I'm not doing that again. Skateboarding is for kids, not adults."

I looked at Dad and said, "Wow, looks like someone needs to work on having a **GONNA-GET-IT-DONE** mindset."

iiiiiiiiiiiiiiiikes!!

29

TIPS for Parents and Educators

When children learn or try something new, they can easily get discouraged when things don't go as planned. They don't yet understand that mistakes and failure are parts of learning. That's why teaching kids how to have a positive, determined mindset is so important. Here are some easy tips to help you teach children how to have a **GONNA-GET-IT-DONE** mindset.

1. Show your child examples of successful people who overcame obstacles in their lives.

2. Praise your child for his or her effort, not just the final outcome.

3. Allow your child to see you work through your struggles.

4. Ask your child one thing he or she wants to improve and then come up with steps to make that happen.

5. Point out areas where your child had struggled but now doesn't.

6. When children say they can't do something, remind them that they might not be able to do it…**YET.** But hard work will pay off!

For more parenting information, visit boystown.org/parenting.

BOYS TOWN® Parenting

Boys Town Press Featured Titles
Kid-friendly books to teach social skills

Executive
FUNction

What Were You Thinking?
Written by Bryan Smith
Illustrated by Lisa M. Griffin

978-1-934490-85-3

Downloadable Activities
Go to BoysTownPress.org to download.

My Day Is Ruined!
A Story for Teaching Flexible Thinking
Written by Bryan Smith
Illustrated by Lisa M. Griffin

978-1-944882-04-4

Of COURSE It's a Big Deal!
A Story about Learning to React Calmly and Appropriately
Written by Bryan Smith
Illustrated by Lisa M. Griffin

978-1-944882-11-2

MINDSET MATTERS
Written by Bryan Smith
Illustrated by Lisa Griffin

978-1-944882-12-9

Is There an App for That?
Written by Bryan Smith
Illustrated by Kalia Wish

Hailey Discovers HAPPiness through Self-Acceptance

978-1-934490-74-7

Is There an App for That? Activity Guide
Written by Bryan Smith
Illustrated by Kalia Wish

Lessons to Teach and Reinforce Self-Acceptance and Positive Changes

978-1-934490-75-4

IF WINNING ISN'T EVERYTHING, WHY DO I HATE TO LOSE?
BRYAN SMITH
Illustrated by BRIAN MARTIN

The National Parenting Center Seal of Approval

978-1-934490-85-3

IF WINNING ISN'T EVERYTHING, WHY DO I HATE TO LOSE?

Lessons to Teach and Reinforce Displaying Good Sportsmanship at School, in Athletics and at Home

978-1-934490-91-4

Kindness Counts
a story for teaching random acts of kindness
Written by Bryan Smith
Illustrated by Brian Martin

978-1-944882-01-3

Downloadable Activities
Go to BoysTownPress.org to download.

BOYS TOWN® Press

For information on Boys Town, its Education Model, Common Sense Parenting®, and training programs:
boystowntraining.org | boystown.org/parenting
training@BoysTown.org | 1-800-545-5771

For parenting and educational books and other resources:
BoysTownPress.org
btpress@BoysTown.org | 1-800-282-6657